The Tree Spot

Written by: Cassandra Troughton

Illustrated by: Nadezhda

Edited by a beautiful friend, Corinne Hansen

This book is dedicated to all the children of Earth (big and small) and the magic that resides within them.
As a child of Earth reading this book, I want to remind you that you are capable of the most powerful of things.
YOU really do have the power to change the world...

And to my special tree spot. The REAL Tree Spot. The tree spot that inspired this story.
Thank you for giving me a safe haven, unconditional love and for filling me with life.
You will forever live on in this book and in my heart.

Copyright© 2024 Cassandra Troughton

All rights reserved. No part of this book may be copied or transmitted in any form or by any means, electronic or mechanical, including photocopying or by any information storage or retrieval system, without the expressed written permission of the publisher.

Ebook: 978-1-7383748-2-3
Paperback: 978-1-7383748-1-6
Hardcover: 978-1-7383748-0-9

mindfulmisst.com
@mindfulmisst
Connect at mindfulmisst@gmail.com

There once was a little child of Earth, named Willow. You could easily pick her out in a crowd; her hair long and wild, and patches of dirt on her rosy cheeks.

Willow looked a little different than the other children of Earth.
And she saw the world a little differently too...
Willow noticed things about the world around her that she just didn't quite understand.

Because of this, Willow spent most of her time alone in her special tree spot.

Every day, she'd wander down to a secluded forest clearing where she looked forward to being surrounded by the magical natural world...

Where all of nature belonged to Willow. And she belonged to nature.

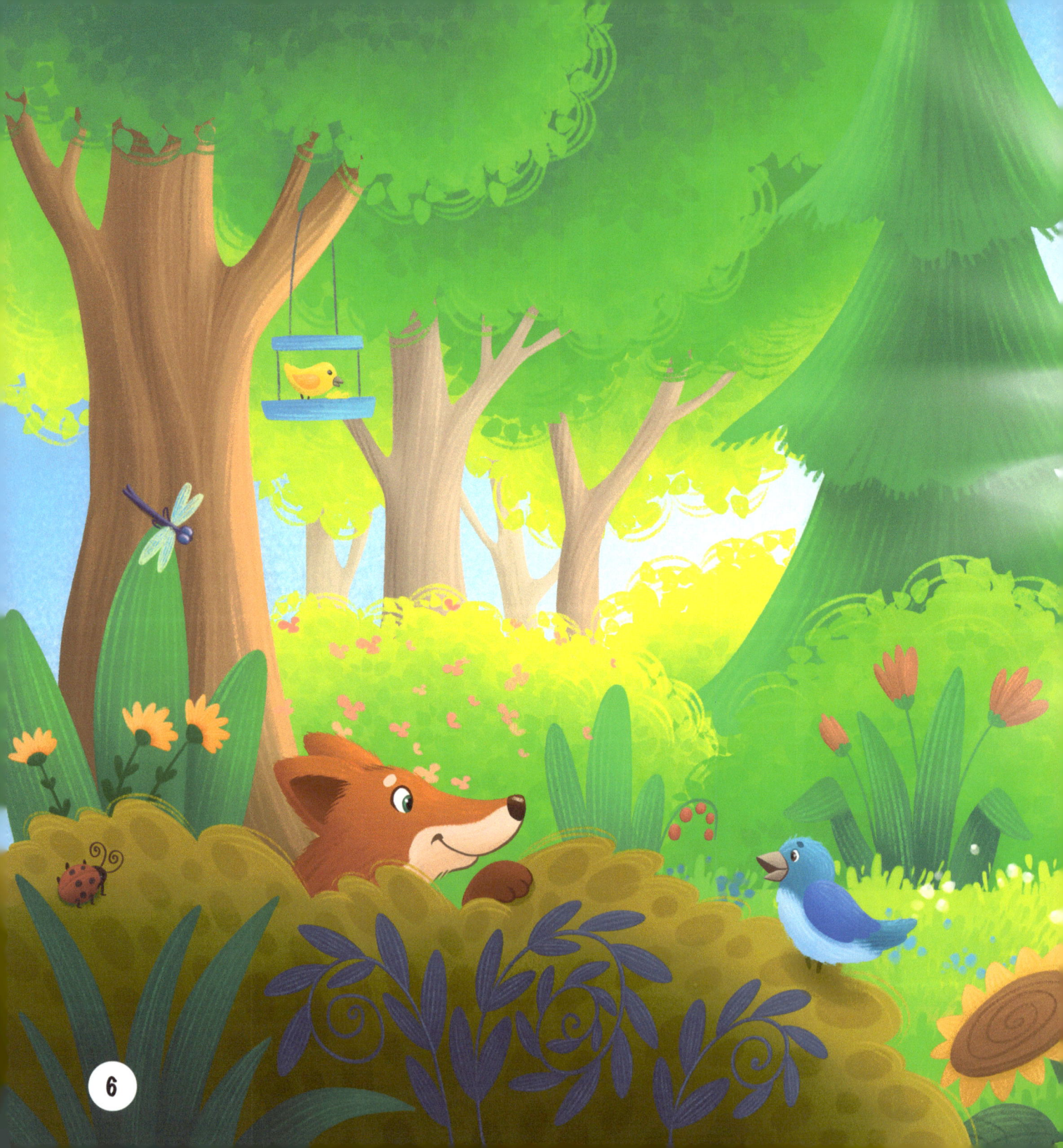

Here, she took care of all the living things, and the living things took care of her too. Everything Willow touched seemed to flourish.

She felt like caring for the creatures of Earth was her calling. It made her heart smile when the flowers blossomed and the birds sang back at her.

She knew then that she had done her job and it was a job that was important for the Earth!

One day, Willow was dancing in her trees when a rustle in the bushes startled her.

She was surprised to see a bronze-skinned Earth boy pop out from behind the bushes.

"Hi, I'm Ari," The boy began to introduce himself, but stopped suddenly as he noticed the living wild behind her, "Wooooooow... what is this place?"

From the Earth boy's perspective, Willow's hidden spot in the trees looked like a dream. He could see that everything was greener here. The colours were vibrant.

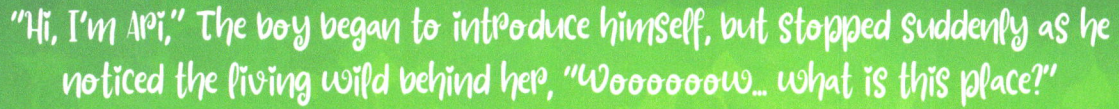

perspective: Point of view. How we see the world through our eyes. Sometimes we can see the world differently than one another, because of our past experiences. It doesn't mean one perspective is right while the other is wrong. It's possible for 2 people to see the same thing differently without either of them being wrong.

"This is my happy place." Willow explained. She began to show Api her way of things.

Willow introduced him to her wild creature friends. She had names for all of them. Even the smallest of creatures.

Then, she picked up a watering can and began showering the plants with nourishment. Api watched intently as her plants happily stretched towards the sky.

Willow walked among the trees and gently embraced each one of them. Api noticed the trees seemed to hug her back.

Ari pet each creature he saw. He even **acknowledged** the ones too small to touch.

Acknowledgment: Noticing and appreciating. Feeling acknowledged and acknowledging others is part of being human. We all need acknowledgment. We all need to feel seen and heard.

Grabbing the watering can from Willow, he watered her flowers, just as she did. Even caressing a few of the petals along the way. His smile grew bigger as he stroked each one.

Ari's eyes seemed to brighten. He looked ahead at the most beautiful tree he'd ever seen. The tree seemed wise somehow and it was as if he could hear it call to him. He bounded towards the tree with open arms.
His embrace was so powerful that the tree began to blush.

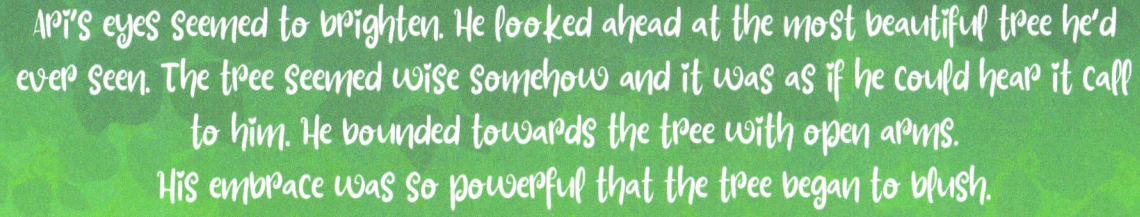

Willow caught the gleam in his eye and saw something warm and loving radiate through his soul. Ari filled with colour.

He was glowing. "Nothing in the city has made me feel like this before. I am so grateful, Willow. Thank you for sharing your tree spot with me."

Grateful: Being thankful and expressing it! To notice the things and people around us and appreciate them by saying thanks. Gratitude is an important feeling for us to feel. It makes us happier and healthier. What is something you're grateful for today?

He gave Willow a quick squeeze and turned to leave, something still glowing inside of him.

Willow was full of joy! Every day, it gave her happiness to care for the Earth and all of the little creatures in her tree spot. But now, sharing her spot with Ari gave her this unusual feeling that she just couldn't explain...

She had never really felt connected to other humans before, only to the Earth. And today, she felt connected to both!

"I wonder how it would feel to share this place with more Earthlings?" she wondered.

Willow never would have imagined what happened next, not even in her wildest dreams...

As soon as Ari left, he couldn't help himself from sharing the magic of Willow's tree spot. When he bumped into a friend on his way home, he told her all about his new friend, Willow.

He went on to share how beautiful the world could be if they all respected and took care of the Earth and all of nature, just like his new friend did.
He told the story of Willow's tree spot and wild friends. A place like no other.
A place where everything was connected and everyone belonged.
A place where everything was one.

Something began glowing in her eyes too. She couldn't believe a place like that really existed. Before she knew it, she was telling her friends, and they were telling their friends, and soon, the message of Willow's tree spot had spread to all of the Earth Children in the city.

They decided they had to see this magical place for themselves.

A few days later, Willow was once again dancing with the wild creatures in her trees when another rustle in the bushes startled her.
This time, the rustle was MUCH louder...

A whole group of little Earthlings emerged! And there was Api, out in front. "Uh... I hope you don't mind Willow, but I told a few friends about you and your magical tree spot. I just wanted them to see the world from your eyes."

Willows lips cracked a gentle smile and she welcomed them in. "It doesn't just have to be my world. It can be all of yours too."

She showed each of them her ways and how to care for the natural world, and in turn, how to care for each other. Reminding them that even humans are a part of nature too.

Each Earth child that had visited Willow's spot brought a piece of the wilderness back with them to the city. They found their own magical tree spots and had their own magical adventures!

And because the children of Earth nurtured the wild things so well, with each passing day, the wilderness spread further and further into the city. And things began to change...

Even the full-grown Earthlings began to be more patient and kind to one another. The wilderness brought peace to the busy city.

Everything around Willow seemed to balance itself out and beings began living in harmony.

No longer disconnected from the world around them.

Acknowledgments

I have an immense amount of gratitude for all who played their parts in this book coming to life. A dedication page was simply not enough to share the love I have for everyone involved. Truth is, some of you may not even know how involved you were in the making of this book. So, it's time that you know...

First and foremost, I want to say thank you to my amazing teaching partner, Kit. In the 4 years we worked together in our little Room 2 classroom, you inspired the heck out of me. This book wouldn't have even been a thought in my mind if it weren't for you sharing your love of picture books with our students and me.

Thank you to my friend, Corinne, for putting on your literacy glasses and looking through my book with your story-loving frame of mind. For proofreading and editing it. For providing suggestions and a second opinion when I needed it most. After looking at the same words on the pages for over 6 years, it became hard to edit. A fresh perspective like yours was appreciated. Thank you for your honest feedback and your unwavering friendship, especially during the toughest of years.

To Pete, my partner for life – thank you for inspiring me to emerge from being a closet writer. For inspiring me and pushing me towards publishing this book! Without your support, help, and listening ear (to the many times I asked you to listen to me read each version of changes), this book would have only held a place in my notebook. Thank you for supporting me in turning my story into a reality.

I have to go way back on this next thank you... To my Elementary School teachers, for instilling a love for writing in me right from the start. I've always had this passion to share stories – to share my story. This passion was fostered well in my youth. There are a select few teachers I know had attributed to this... This is my thank you to you. You all did one heck of a job in giving this student the skills and passion to bring stories to life.

Thank you to my parents for also instilling a love of books in me. And for encouraging me to get outside and play as a child – to connect with nature. Most importantly, thank you for taking me outside of the city and giving me my own forest of trees. I don't know if you ever truly understood how those trees saved me... For that, I am eternally grateful for you both. That experience and this book wouldn't have been possible without you.

Thank you to my sister, Jaclyn. I know I wasn't always the best sister growing up, or even the best role model, but thank you for following me to the ends of the Earth when we were kids. Thank you for exploring nature with me. For all of our outdoor adventures and imaginative play. For all of the hideaway places we found in the trees – as kids and now again as adults. I don't know if I would have felt as connected to nature if I didn't have you there to explore the outdoors with me. Thank you forever.

And finally...

To my acreage. It was here where I got to connect so closely to nature every single day. It was here that I found my little tree spot in the woods. Although it felt completely random and out of the ordinary that a born and raised city slicker like myself moved an hour outside of the city and found peace in a small town, I know that there are no such things as coincidences. Something drew me out there... I felt this immense pull deep in my heart. I knew that it was here where I truly belonged. As much as it saddens me to know that most of the land there has been destroyed, including my tree spot, and that my little 100 year old converted train station home sits abandoned in the middle of an industrial zone, I am just so grateful that I got the opportunity to meet you when I did. That I got the opportunity know every hill and every dip on this land like the back of my hand. That I got to experience your beauty. And grateful that I got to hold you in my heart for as long as I did.

I guess one final thank you is in order...

Thank you universe for allowing my life unfold the way it did. For leading me out into the country and for leading me to a blank page where this book first began...

About the Author

Cassandra Troughton

Cassandra Troughton, is a former elementary educator, and current writer, from Wabamun, Alberta, Canada. She brings her passion for nature and storytelling to the world of children's literature with her picture book, "The Tree Spot." With seven years of experience in Edmonton Public Schools (a.k.a. Seven years of experience of reading picture books to students), Cassandra has dedicated her career to nurturing young souls, and inspiring them through story.

Now, an online content and copywriter who writes picture books for fun, she channels her creativity into stories that hold powerful messages for both children and adults. "The Tree Spot," began as a passion project in 2016. She felt inspired to write a story about her very own spot out in nature – a place on her acreage where she found solace among her trees. Her connection to nature and subsequent loss of this Tree Spot in 2017 deeply influenced the book's narrative, weaving a story of love, connection, and resilience.

When not immersed in her writing, Cassandra can be found with her nose in between a book, hiking the Nelson mountains in her new hometown, snuggling up with her pets, dancing her heart out, and advocating for mindfulness. A lifelong learner, she continues to share her knowledge and insights with people of all ages, fostering a community of mindful living and learning.

About the Illustrator

Nadezhda

My path to the profession of book illustrator was not an easy one.

Early in my career, I worked for a local television station editing commercials and news programs. And sometimes wedding movies.

At that time I was drawing a little bit, but it was just a hobby. Until I got into the computer game industry. Those few years were very exciting! I worked as a 2D artist, doing visual effects for games.

After living in several big cities, I returned to my small provincial Barnaul. Only after the birth of my first son did I realize what I was really interested in. Illustrating children's books! The opportunity to realize the author's idea, putting a part of your soul into it - is it not magic? When a barely comprehensible sketch turns into a small mouse or a huge fire-breathing dragon!

Now that I have three sons and over 20 illustrated books, I continue to draw. Watching my children grow up has only increased my love of children's illustration. And I am grateful for the opportunity to bring joy to young readers.

Book design credits: Kay Ray at GetYourBookIllustrations

www.ingramcontent.com/pod-product-compliance
Lightning Source LLC
Chambersburg PA
CBHW041528070526
44585CB00003B/120